This book belongs to:

....

Granny Bouncer's Rescue

Written and Illustrated by
John Patience

DERRYDALE BOOKS
New York
© Fern Hollow Productions Ltd:
Peter Haddock Ltd., U.K.
This 1984 edition is published by Derrydale Books,
distributed by Crown Publishers, Inc.
Printed in Italy
ISBN 0-517-457989
hgfedcba

The day for the annual seaside trip had arrived and Fern Hollow railroad station was packed with excited animals buying tickets, showing off new buckets and spades and exclaiming to each other what a perfectly beautiful day it was. As was usual for this occasion, a special train had been booked and, as it drew into the station puffing out steam and smoke, an enormous cheer went up from the children.

7

8

Eventually everyone got themselves settled in the train and were impatient to be off, but there was a problem. Granny Bouncer had not yet arrived. "Perhaps she isn't well," some animals suggested. "Maybe she has forgotten about the trip," others said. At last, just as the train was about to leave without her, Granny came running down the platform. "I forgot my knitting," she panted, waving a multicolored object on the end of her needles. "I had to go back for it."

9

The guard blew his whistle and Mr. Rusty, the engine driver, started the train. Soon they were rushing through the open countryside. The children looked out of the windows. There was a lot to see: a scarecrow, a windmill and a canal with lots of little boats on it. Meanwhile Granny Bouncer

concentrated on her knitting, occasionally pausing to pop a candy into her mouth. Suddenly, the train puffed round the side of a hill and there was the sea, all sparkling and blue in the morning sunshine!

At Brineybeach Station the animals bustled out of their carriages and sniffed the air. It was filled with the wonderful, exciting smell of the sea. Soon everyone was down on the beach. The children and some of the more daring older animals changed into their bathing suits. Some went for a paddle or a swim in the sea. Others watched the Punch and Judy show.

The children began to build sand castles and a competition was held to choose the best one. It was won by Jiggy and Jasper Acorn, whose castle was at least twice as big as the others and had lots of little flags stuck into it. Unfortunately, later in the afternoon, the tide began to come in and washed the castle away. Then Jasper began to cry, but he was soon cheered up when Mr. Acorn bought him an ice cream cone.

At last the sun began to slip down on the horizon and the air
grew cooler. Then everyone changed out of their bathing
suits back into their warm clothes. It was decided at this
point that they would all go for a walk along the pier. Granny
Bouncer went along too, but she quickly found a deck chair
and got on with her knitting. She had been busy all afternoon
and had produced a very, very, very long scarf.

18

Pippa Bouncer climbed onto the pier railings and sat her teddy bear on them so that it could look at the sea. Then something terrible happened. The teddy bear slipped out of Pippa's hands and, as she made a grab for it, she fell off the pier and splashed down into the sea. There was a general panic on the pier with no one knowing what to do. Then Granny Bouncer came to the rescue. She lowered one end of her enormous scarf down to Pippa who, of course, grabbed it and held on hard. "Heave-ho!" cried Granny, and everyone hauled Pippa up to safety. The poor little rabbit was rather wet and frightened, but otherwise quite all right.

It had been a very eventful day, but now it was time to go home. The train journey back to Fern Hollow was not as exciting as the one they had made that morning, but everyone was feeling happy and contented. Most of the

children fell asleep while the adults chatted about the day's events. As for Granny Bouncer, all that could be heard from her was the clicking of her knitting needles!

Fern Hollow

MR CHIPS'S HOUSE

MR. WILLOWBANK'S
COBBLER'S SHOP

MR CROAKER'S WATERMILL

STRIPEY'S HOUSE

SCHOOL

RIVER FERNY

THE JOLLY VOLE
HOTEL

MR. RUSTY'S HOUSE

MR ACORN'S
BAKERY

MR PRICKLES'S HOUSE

POST OFFICE

BORIS BLINKS'S
BOOKSHOP

MR TWINKLE'S
HOUSE

MR TUTTLEEBEE'S
SHOP

MR THIMBLE'S
TAILORS SHOP

WINDYWOOD